TOADS AND FROGS

BY M. J. YORK

Published by The Child's World®
1980 Lookout Drive • Mankato, MN 56003-1705
800-599-READ • www.childsworld.com

Photographs ©: Serg Bimbirekov/Shutterstock Images, cover (toad), 3, 8, 20, 24 (toad); Shuttestock Images, cover (frog), 2, 15, 21, 24 (frog); KWS Photography/Shutterstock Images, 5; Natalia Baran/Shutterstock Images, 6; Patrick K. Campbell/Shutterstock Images, 9; David Byron Keener/Shutterstock Images, 10; Klaus Ulrich Mueller/Shutterstock Images, 13; Dave M. Hunt Photography/Shutterstock Images, 14; iStockphoto, 17; Pavel Kransensky/Shutterstock Images, 19

ISBN 9781503835863
LCCN 2019943002

Printed in the United States of America

ABOUT THE AUTHOR

M. J. York is a children's author and editor living in Minnesota. She loves learning about different animals.

TABLE OF CONTENTS

CHAPTER

1

Leggy Amphibian

An **amphibian** sits on a rock near a pond. Its long legs are folded under its body. Suddenly its tongue shoots from its mouth. It snags a fly. Lunchtime! Is this hungry creature a toad or a frog? How are they different?

Amphibians such as frogs usually live near water.

Some people believe touching a toad can cause warts, but this is not true.

CHAPTER

2

Toads

Toads have warty, bumpy skin. Most have dull colors. Their skin looks dry. Toads can spend periods of time away from water. Many have poison **glands** behind their eyes. The glands make a milky liquid that burns **predators**. Many toads puff themselves up so predators can't swallow them.

Toads have short, fat bodies. Their heads are round. Their toes are not usually **webbed**. They are not good jumpers. Their legs are good for short hops and for digging.

Cane toads are from Central and South America, but they have spread to other places including Australia and parts of the United States.

Toads dig **burrows** with their back legs. They sleep through the winter in these burrows.

Toad eggs are kept in long, clear tubes of jelly.

Most toads lay eggs in water. The eggs are closed in long tubes of jelly. There can be thousands of eggs in each long line! The eggs hatch into tadpoles. The tadpoles later change into toads. But some kinds of toads lay eggs on land. These hatch into small toads. A few toads do not lay eggs at all. Their babies are born from their bodies.

CHAPTER

3

Frogs

Frogs have smooth skin. Some are brownish and greenish. Others have bright colors. Their skin looks shiny. Frogs stay near water. They need to keep their skin wet. Some frogs make poison under their skin.

Many brightly colored frogs are poisonous to predators.

Some people build ponds in their gardens for frogs to live in.

Frogs have thinner bodies than toads. Their heads are pointed. Very long legs make them good jumpers. Many have webbed toes on their back legs. This helps them swim. Tree frogs use sticky pads on their front toes for climbing.

Some frogs **survive** winter underwater. Others hide in leaves. A type of sugar in their bodies lets them freeze without dying. They thaw in spring and wake up. Frogs lay eggs in water. They lay eggs in bunches like grapes.

Many frogs survive being frozen in the winter.

CHAPTER

4

What's the Difference?

Toads have bumpy, dry skin and short legs for digging. They can live away from water. Frogs have smooth, moist skin and long legs for jumping. They stay close to water.

Toads can be found on every continent except Antarctica.

There are many types of toads and frogs. They are all closely related. Some have features of both frogs and toads. Some toads are smooth. Some frogs live in dry places. But they are all exciting!

TOADS

- Take short hops
- Spend the winter in burrows
- Lay eggs in long tubes

FROGS

- Good jumpers
- Freeze during the winter
- Lay eggs in bunches

GLOSSARY

amphibian (am-FIB-ee-uhn) An amphibian is an animal that lives the first part of its life in the water and moves to land as an adult. A frog is an amphibian.

burrows (BUR-rowz) Burrows are holes or tunnels made by animals for shelter. Toads dig burrows where they sleep through the winter.

glands (GLANDZ) Glands are body parts that make chemicals or liquids. Toads have glands that make poison.

predators (PRED-uh-turs) Predators are animals that hunt and eat other animals. Toads make poison to protect themselves from predators.

survive (sur-VIVE) To survive is to live. Some frogs survive through the winter by staying underwater.

webbed (WEBD) Something that is webbed is connected by a thin fold of skin. Frogs have webbed feet.

TO LEARN MORE

IN THE LIBRARY

Amstutz, Lisa J. *Amazing Amphibians: 30 Activities and Observations for Exploring Frogs, Toads, Salamanders, and More*. Chicago, IL: Chicago Review Press, 2020.

An, Vickie. *Amphibian Rescue*. Huntington Beach, CA: Teacher Created Materials, 2018.

Mattern, Joanne. *Frogs and Toads*. Egremont, MA: Red Chair Press, 2017.

ON THE WEB

Visit our website for links about toads and frogs:

childsworld.com/links

Note to Parents, Teachers, and Librarians: We routinely verify our Web links to make sure they are safe and active sites. So encourage your readers to check them out!

ACTIVITY

Draw a picture of a toad and a frog. Your picture should clearly show the differences between the toad and the frog. Look at pages 20 and 21 for help.

INDEX